Ten Beautiful Things

Molly Beth Griffin • *Illustrated by* **Maribel Lechuga**

ini Charlesbridge

For my mom, a great inventor of car games—M. B. G.
To my husband, my best traveling companion—M. L.

At the time of publication, all URLs printed in this book were accurate and active. Charlesbridge, the author, and the illustrator are not responsible for the content or accessibility of any website.

Published by Charlesbridge
9 Galen Street
Watertown, MA 02472
(617) 926-0329 • www.charlesbridge.com

Printed in China
(hc) 10 9 8 7 6 5 4 3 2

Illustrations done in Photoshop and Clip Studio Paint, with added watercolor textures
    made in traditional mediums
Display type set in Desire by Charles Borges de Oliveira
Text type set in Adobe Caslon Pro by Adobe Systems Incorporated
Color separations by Colourscan Print Co Pte Ltd, Singapore
Printed by 1010 Printing International Limited in Huizhou, Guangdong, China
Production supervision by Brian G. Walker
Designed by Jacqueline Noelle Cote

Library of Congress Cataloging-in-Publication Data
Names: Griffin, Molly Beth, author.
Title: Ten beautiful things/Molly Beth Griffin.
Description: Watertown, MA: Charlesbridge, [2021] | Summary: Lily is moving into her grandmother's farm in Iowa, and she is sad about all the changes necessary in her life—but on the long drive her grandmother challenges her to find ten beautiful things that they can share together.
Identifiers: LCCN 2019014524 (print) | LCCN 2019020549 (ebook) | ISBN 9781580899369 (hardcover) | ISBN 9781632897909 (ebook)
Subjects: LCSH: Life change events—Juvenile fiction. | Grandmothers—Juvenile fiction. | Grandparent and child—Juvenile fiction. | Loss (Psychology)—Juvenile fiction. | Iowa—Juvenile fiction. | CYAC: Moving, Household—Fiction. | Grandmothers—Fiction. | Automobile travel—Fiction. | Loss (Psychology)—Fiction. | Iowa—Fiction.
Classification: LCC PZ7.G8813593 Te 2021 (print) | LCC PZ7. G8813593 (ebook) | DDC [E]—dc23
LC record available at https://lccn.loc.gov/2019014524
LC ebook record available at https://lccn.loc.gov/2019020549

Lily ran her finger across the Iowa map.
An X marked Gram's house
on an empty patch of land.
Lily's new home.

Gram's car tires hummed against the pavement.
Lily felt the vibration in her hollow chest.
"Let's try to find ten beautiful things
along the way," Gram said.

Lily turned her eyes to the window.
"There's nothing beautiful here," she said.
She struggled to fold the map
so it nestled into itself just right.

"You'd be surprised," Gram said.

And sure enough, at that very moment,
the sun broke over the long horizon.

Lily gasped.
"There's number one!" she cried.
"Right you are, Lily," said Gram.

Fence posts rushed past.
Gram flipped on the radio,
trying to fill the silence.

Lily felt the complaints
starting in her belly again,
coming up her throat
and nearly out her mouth.

But then Gram shouted,
"Number two!"

A wind farm had sprouted
in the field beside the freeway.
Spinning windmill blades
gleamed in the morning sun.

Lily concentrated on the game and found
number three real fast—a red-winged blackbird
perched on a swaying stalk of last year's corn.
It was dark and bright all at once,
its beak wide open in a song they couldn't hear.

Later Gram signaled and turned the car
onto a smaller road.
"Two more highways to go," she said.
Lily popped a handful of crackers into her mouth,
but food didn't fill up her hollow places.
Gram cracked her window,
and in rushed air and sound and cold.

They crossed a bridge,
and Gram chose number four—
the gurgly sound of a melting creek.

Lily dozed off.
She woke up when Gram tapped her knee
and pointed out a falling-apart barn.
"That's not pretty," Lily said. "That can't count."

"We're not looking for pretty.
We want *beautiful,*" Gram said.
So it stood. Halfway to ten.

At a rest area Lily bounced out of the car,
while Gram stretched her creaky body.
Lily picked number six.
"The smell of mud," she said, inhaling.
Gram shut her eyes and nodded slowly.
"It's earthy and rich," she said.
"I'd never really noticed."

Lily breathed in the mud smell
and focused on just that.
It poured itself into some of the empty spaces in her.

Back on the road again, the car seemed smaller.
The humming in Lily had stopped,
but her legs wanted to sprawl,
and her stomach was getting queasy.

"We're on a roll now," Gram said,
and she was right about that.
Seven and eight were easy:
a cloud shaped like a swan,
and a little brown calf that trotted beside the fence.

Miles and miles later they turned onto their last road,
and the clouds began to draw close.
The sky grew dark. The earth rumbled.
Suddenly the air exploded in bright flashes.
Cloud banks traded lightning back and forth,
showing off.

"Number nine," Lily whispered.
There was no room for other words.

The storm took up the whole world,
and it filled Lily up, too.
She was here, with Gram,
and for a whole minute
that was all that mattered.

On they drove. *Almost there. Not far now.*

When they'd been *almost* there for a long time,
Gram braked, eased the car
down a crumbling driveway,
and parked in front of the farmhouse.

"Here we be," she said,
through the drum of the rain. "Home."
"But we only made it to nine," Lily said,
slumping in her seat.

"Nope. Ten, easy."
Gram came around with the umbrella,
and Lily stepped out of the car.

"*We're* ten," Gram said.

Lily sank into her familiar hug.

None of this was easy.

Maybe it would never be easy.

But she belonged with Gram now.

She belonged *here* now.

This place wasn't empty,
and neither was she.